THE BATTLE

Contents

Badger
L E A R N I N G

Characters

Ron Grant

Alex Cook (Cookie)

Callum

Jorge Alvarez

Angelo

Jackson

Mani Gronier

Jadon Brooks

Bradle

Marissa

THE
BATTLE

Written by Alan Durant
Illustrated by Will Huck

Thanks to Inclusive Minds (the CIC supporting and championing inclusion and diversity in children's books) for introducing us to Kay and Gabriella through their network of Inclusion Ambassadors.

Special thanks also to Harrison, Parker and Reegan.

Titles in the Making the Team Series:

The Challenge

The Battle

Up and Running

Paying the Penalty

Taking a Stand

The Final

Badger Publishing Limited
Oldmedow Road,
Hardwick Industrial Estate,
King's Lynn PE30 4JJ

Telephone: **01553 816 082**
www.badgerlearning.co.uk

2 4 6 8 10 9 7 5 3 1

The Battle
ISBN 978-1-78837-656-3

Text © Alan Durant 2022
Illustration © Will Huck 2022
Complete work © Badger Publishing Limited 2022

Commissioning Editor: Sarah Rudd
Editor: Claire Morgan
Designer: Bigtop Design
Cover: alphaspirit.it/Shutterstock

THE
BATTLE

Written by Alan Durant
Illustrated by Will Huck

Thanks to Inclusive Minds (the CIC supporting and championing inclusion and diversity in children's books) for introducing us to Kay and Gabriella through their network of Inclusion Ambassadors.

Special thanks also to Harrison, Parker and Reegan.

WITHDRAWN

Titles in the Making the Team Series:

The Challenge

The Battle

Up and Running

Paying the Penalty

Taking a Stand

The Final

Badger Publishing Limited
Oldmedow Road,
Hardwick Industrial Estate,
King's Lynn PE30 4JJ

Telephone: **01553 816 082**
www.badgerlearning.co.uk

2 4 6 8 10 9 7 5 3 1

The Battle
ISBN 978-1-78837-656-3

Commissioning Editor: Sarah Rudd
Editor: Claire Morgan
Designer: Bigtop Design
Cover: alphaspirit.it/Shutterstock

byline: the boundary lines at either end of the football pitch

deflection: when a player gets in the way of the ball and it bounces off them

digs: housing

full back: a defensive player, usually positioned near the side of the pitch

infield: away from the touchlines and towards the penalty box

marker: someone who is trying to stop an opposing team member from receiving the ball

pre-season: the time before official matches start, involving training and friendly matches

scholarship: an amount of money given by a school to a student to support their learning/development

CHAPTER ONE

Jackson Mbemba looked over the balcony outside his parents' flat.

They lived on the third floor and the view wasn't great.

Looking down, he could see the huge round bins where everyone on the estate put their rubbish. The bins were overfull and surrounded by plastic bags of extra rubbish.

It was a mess.

A young woman was carrying a small crying child across the cracked concrete.

Somewhere out of sight, a man and a woman were swearing loudly at each other.

Two figures lurked in a gloomy doorway. Members of the estate gang, no doubt.

Jackson hated this place.

His parents had moved the family here four years ago when Jackson was signed by Stanford Academy. Before that, they had lived in London where Jackson was at the Charlton Academy.

Jackson knew that Stanford was a step up — they were a Premier League club — but he missed London. He missed his friends and he missed the estate where he used to live. People were so friendly there. They were always in and out of each other's flats and they shared what they had.

Here, the estate looked similar but the people couldn't be more different.

Jackson was only on the estate on Sundays now. The rest of the week he stayed in digs nearer the Stanford ground with a woman called Mrs Earls, who had looked after a lot of young footballers.

Mrs Earls said Jackson was better off away from the estate. It was trouble, she said.

And she was right.

The gang made trouble for everyone. That's why Jackson had to make it as a footballer — to get his family out of this dump. His mum and dad had worked so hard and given up so much for him. Now, it was time to pay them back.

Jackson had been delighted when the manager, Ron Grant, had told him that he'd made the First Team squad for the pre-season tournament. But that was just the start.

Jackson needed to make an impression, to grab this chance by the scruff of the neck and win the pro contract that would change his life. His whole family's lives.

Jackson was three and his sister, Marissa, was just a baby when they left their home in the Congo to come to England as refugees.

Jackson's dad had spoken out against the government and his life was in danger. They had to leave.

Jackson's dad was a teacher in the Congo but he found it hard to get a job in England. Now, he was a bus driver.

Jackson's mum worked at the local supermarket and took on ironing work in the evenings. She always found the time, though, to make sure that Jackson and his sister ate properly — and did their homework!

Marissa was also into football. She was part of the Stanford women's squad, but she and Jackson were only allowed to play as long as they kept up with their studies.

"A good education is the most precious gift in life," Mum once told them sternly. Then she smiled. "And, besides, even footballers need brains, don't they?"

Jackson's mum loved football. When she was a girl, she had always joined in the kickabouts with the local boys.

She was so pleased when Jackson had signed a scholarship contract with Stanford when he was 16.

Jackson's dad wasn't so interested in football. His game was chess. He would play for hours with his mates down at the social club. He was proud of his son's sporting achievements, but Jackson knew his dad was prouder that he'd got eight GCSEs and three A-levels.

Jackson was proud of that too, but right now, it was his football skills that needed to shine. He'd done well so far. Now it was time to take his play up to another level.

CHAPTER TWO

"Come on, speed up! This is like an old-age pensioners' picnic," bellowed the coach.

Stanford's First Team coach, Alex Cook, nicknamed Cookie, was in a bad mood and letting his players know it. He was giving everyone a hard time. Even captain Jadon Brooks got a telling off for not moving the ball quickly enough.

The young players didn't escape Cookie's tongue either.

Callum had "the ball control of a drunk donkey".

Angelo was "so laid back he was almost asleep".

Jackson "couldn't tackle the skin off a rice pudding".

"Just ignore Cookie's insults," Jadon Brooks told the three young players at the end of the session. "His bark is worse than his bite. He's always like this just before a match."

Jackson nodded. To be honest, it hadn't really worried him. He knew his game and that he was good at it. If he was selected to play in the first match of the tournament, then he'd be ready.

He could see that the other two had been affected though, especially Angelo. He was a brilliant player and could turn a match around with his skill, but his confidence was easily knocked.

Callum wasn't the best player technically, but he scored goals for fun.

All three of them were in the squad on merit.

They just needed to prove it to Cookie.

*

That afternoon, Jackson worked harder than ever in the gym.

He had a great 'engine', as all his academy coaches told him, but he could always be fitter and stronger. Jackson's skill was breaking up the play and then sprinting forwards to support the attack, so he needed more energy than anyone else.

It was all right for Callum. He just had to hang about up front waiting for the ball to come his way, but Jackson had to hunt it down.

Jackson's hero was N'Golo Kanté. When Kanté was on the pitch, Jackson studied him like he was one of his exam subjects.

Lots of people thought that footballers were stupid, that their brains were in their feet, but that wasn't true. You needed plenty of brains to be one step ahead of your opponent, and you needed peak fitness to stay there.

It was the mix of brains and fitness that had made Jackson the Under-21 captain at 18. He wasn't loud on the pitch. He didn't shout at other players. He tried to lead by example.

Jason Smith, the Under-21 coach, said he was the right choice for captain because all the players respected him. Jackson felt proud when he heard that.

Jackson's dad was like that. He was calm and quiet, but he had strong beliefs and he wasn't afraid to show them, even if they put his life in danger. People respected him, and to Jackson's dad, that was the most important thing in life.

Jackson carried that thought into every game. He played as if his life was in danger, as if he was in a battle.

Well, it turned out that the next day, he was.

CHAPTER THREE

It started like any ordinary day.

Jackson woke up early as usual and ate the healthy breakfast Mrs Earls had made for him: lots of fruit with plain yoghurt, two boiled eggs and a large glass of milk. Jackson didn't drink tea or coffee, but he loved milk.

Then he set off for the club.

Jackson could see from the nearly empty car park that he was one of the first to arrive. As he reached the entrance, a silver Range Rover pulled up with the number plate MAN1.

It was Mani Gronier, Stanford's midfield enforcer and one of the hardest players in the league. He liked to show off — hence the number plate.

When Jackson got his pro contract, the first thing he was going to do was buy an expensive car. Not for himself. He hadn't even passed his test yet. It would be for his parents.

Then his dad could get rid of that rusty old Nissan Micra he drove — when it worked!

Jackson went straight to the gym.

Callum was already there because he did a session before training every morning to get himself fitter. He needed it too.

Callum was on his back doing bench presses when Jackson walked in. His face was red with effort.

"Morning, mate," Jackson greeted his teammate. He raised an eyebrow. "You look... warm."

Callum hooked the bar into its rest and sat up. He shook his head.

"If only there was an easier way to get fit," Callum sighed.

"No pain, no gain," said Jackson, smiling.

Callum got up and Jackson took his place on the bench.

"Now, let me show you how it's really done," teased Jackson.

Callum laughed. Jackson was in much better shape than him and made the bench presses look easy.

Callum admired Jackson and hoped he could reach the same fitness level one day.

"Have fun, don't push yourself too hard," Callum said, as he walked off to take a shower.

*

There was nothing unusual about the training drills that day.

As ever, Jackson was one of the first to complete the hurdles and sprints. His short passing was sharp, his long passing was accurate and his control was almost perfect.

His shooting wasn't great, but then it never was. No one really expected it to be. His job was to give other players the chance to shoot.

The session ended with a thirty-minute match.

Normally this would be six or seven-aside, but today Cookie wanted a full eleven-aside match.

Cookie had already picked the sides. It looked to Jackson like it was the A team versus the B team — First Team against the reserves, and he was a reserve!

Cookie had set up a whiteboard and he drew lines and arrows to explain the tactics he wanted both sides to use.

"I want the ball kept on the floor as much as possible," he said. "I don't want to see any players sitting back and being lazy. Treat this like a proper match."

He didn't need to tell Jackson that. Every game was a proper match for him.

Let the battle commence...

CHAPTER FOUR

The First Team started well.

Mani Gronier was running things in midfield and it was from his pass that the First Team striker, Reegan Keller, opened the scoring.

Jackson was running around, but he felt like he was chasing shadows. He couldn't get hold of the ball.

Gronier was brilliant, making tackles, playing passes. It was only a matter of time before the second goal came.

Gronier won the ball from Angelo and set up Keller again. This time, the striker's shot would have gone wide, but it took a huge deflection off a defender's knee, giving the goalie no chance.

2–0 to the First Team.

This wasn't going how Jackson had hoped. He needed to do something if he was going to get on the starting team for the tournament, and he needed to do it quickly.

It was time for him to use his brains. It didn't take a genius to see what needed to be done: stop Gronier.

From the kick-off, Jackson moved himself a little further up the field, so that he was opposite Gronier. The next time the midfielder received the ball, Jackson was on him.

WHAM!

His tackle not only took the ball, but took Gronier's legs too.

"Argh!" cried Gronier, muttering something in French which sounded like swearing.

He got to his feet angrily, looking for the ref to call a foul, but the game played on.

The next time Gronier got the ball, Jackson stepped in carefully but quickly and gained possession of the ball.

He sprinted to the byline and whipped in a cross towards Callum. Callum diverted it into the path of veteran striker, Jorge Alvarez, who crashed the ball into the net.

2-1.

Jackson looked across at the touchline and saw Ron Grant standing there. It made him even more determined. He had to make an impression.

He stayed tight to Gronier, making him rush his passes. Each time Jackson made a tackle he could hear Gronier mutter in angry frustration.

Gronier was used to being top dog and he didn't like things not going his way.

Jackson was happy his plan was working, but he wanted more. He wanted to show that there was more to his game than just stopping his opponent.

The next time the ball was played towards Gronier, Jackson moved swiftly and cut in to take the ball. Then he sprinted forwards, leaving the French star far behind him.

As he approached the First Team's penalty area, Jackson pretended to pass to Brooks, then swivelled and slipped the ball the other way to Callum.

Callum reached the ball an instant before his marker and slid it into the corner of the net.

2–2!

Gronier glared at Jackson as he passed him on the way back to the centre of the pitch. He spat on the ground and said something in French.

Jackson knew enough French to understand he was being racially abused, but he ignored it. Although it made him angry, Jackson knew a confrontation on the pitch would not go well. He would decide what to do about it later.

Right now, all he wanted to do was win this match.

The game was almost over but the battle was just about to begin.

At the next kick-off, the ball was booted forwards and out of play.

Angelo took the throw-in. He threw the ball back to his full back, who passed infield to Jackson, facing towards his own goal.

Jackson controlled the ball and started to turn when...

WHOOSH!

Jackson's legs were taken from under him, flipping him backwards. He landed with a thump on the ground.

Jackson lay on his back, winded and dazed. He was aware of shouting above him and glanced up to see Alvarez aim a punch at Gronier.

Jackson heard a sickening thud and watched Gronier fall to the ground.

After that, all hell broke loose.

Players from both sides rushed over to get involved — some wanting to fight, some wanting to stop the fighting.

Cookie pushed his way in among the players, roaring for everyone to stop. He looked livid.

"HEY! STOP THIS! You're supposed to be teammates!" barked Cookie.

He bent over Jackson. "Are you okay, lad?"

Jackson sat up and nodded. He got to his feet. He seemed to be all right. Mani Gronier was up as well and was rubbing his jaw.

"Everyone inside. Now," Cookie growled.

CHAPTER FIVE

The squad was called together in the players' lounge. Ron Grant was glowing with rage.

"I won't have brawling at this club," he shouted. "Alvarez and Gronier, I want you both in my office after this meeting."

The two players nodded. Mani Gronier still looked furious, but Jorge Alvarez seemed calm and relaxed.

Jackson liked Alvarez. He was the club's record goal scorer and a legend, but he always had time for the young players. He'd spent ages helping Callum.

The manager took a deep breath. He seemed calmer.

"Now, I'm going to announce the team to start our first match in the tournament," said Grant. "As you know, there are eight international teams taking part — two groups of four with the winners going into the final. We've been drawn with Sevilla, Porto and AC Milan. First up is Sevilla."

Jackson's mind was racing. Sevilla! Porto! AC Milan! Three top European teams. And he had a chance of playing in a game against them.

He hoped what had happened with Gronier wouldn't count against him. He really didn't want Grant to think he was a troublemaker.

Jackson wanted to be respected as someone who was calm and composed, just like his father. It was critical that players could keep their cool on the pitch and their focus on the game.

Hopefully Grant could see that Jackson wasn't going to react like Gronier.

"I'm announcing the team a day early," Grant continued, "because it's our first pre-season game and I want you to have plenty of time to prepare."

He held up a sheet of paper.

Jackson's heart thumped. He could see the writing through the paper, but he couldn't read the names.

He'd just have to wait and hope.

Even a place on the bench would be a dream come true.

Jackson had worked so hard to prove himself. He hoped he had done enough. But even if he hadn't, at least he knew he had given it everything.

Ron Grant read out the names: goalie, full backs, centre backs, midfield, wide players, striker...

Jackson's name wasn't called but he hadn't expected it to be. Now for the subs.

But wait... Grant had only read out ten names.

"My final pick is midfield and I've left it until last because it was a tough decision. But I've decided to give an opportunity to a young man with a bright future."

Grant turned his gaze on Jackson. "That's you, Jackson," he said, smiling. "Well done, son."

Jackson looked at Grant in shock. Had he really just called his name? He felt stunned as he turned to look at the other players.

Jorge Alvarez started clapping and the rest of the team joined in. Jackson grinned. His heart felt like it was bursting with happiness.

He'd done it. He was in the team!

Jackson was still on a high when he walked out of the club half an hour later with Callum and Angelo. They had been named as subs so they were happy too.

They ambled across the car park, chatting excitedly. They passed Mani Gronier's silver Range Rover.

Arriving that morning, Jackson had been in awe of Gronier. Now, he'd replaced him in the team.

So much had changed in a few hours. Jackson couldn't wait to tell Marissa and his mum and dad. He'd done it! He'd won the battle.

Now, for the war.

Roll on Saturday and Sevilla!

Further activities

1. It kicks off in more ways than one during this story! Write an engaging blog entry from the point of view of a spectator who watched the fight unfold during training.

2. Ron Grant chooses his team for the Sevilla match very carefully. Who would your football dream team be and why?

Enjoyed this book?

Follow the Making the Team journey
across all six brilliant stories!